RETOLD BY Carl Bowen, Michael Dahl, Louise Simonson
ART BY Eduardo Garcia, Tod Smith, Rex Lokus

GODS AND THUNDER

A GRAPHIC NOVEL OF OLD NORSE MYTHS

Capstone Young Readers
a capstone imprint

Gods and Thunder is published by
Capstone Young Readers
A Capstone Imprint
1710 Roe Crest Drive
North Mankato, Minnesota 56003
www.mycapstone.com

Cataloging-in-Publication Data is available at the Library of Congress website.
ISBN: 978-1-62370-848-1 (paperback)
ISBN: 978-1-62370-849-8 (e-book)

Summary: A collection of Norse myths brought to life in graphic novel format. Tales include Thor and Loki's journey into the mysterious giant city Utgard, the exploits of Thor as he battles and outwits three giants, the death of the beloved god Baldur, and the unfolding of Ragnarök, the end of the world.

Editors: Aaron Sautter and Abby Huff
Designers: Kristi Carlson and Bob Lentz
Production Specialist: Laura Manthe

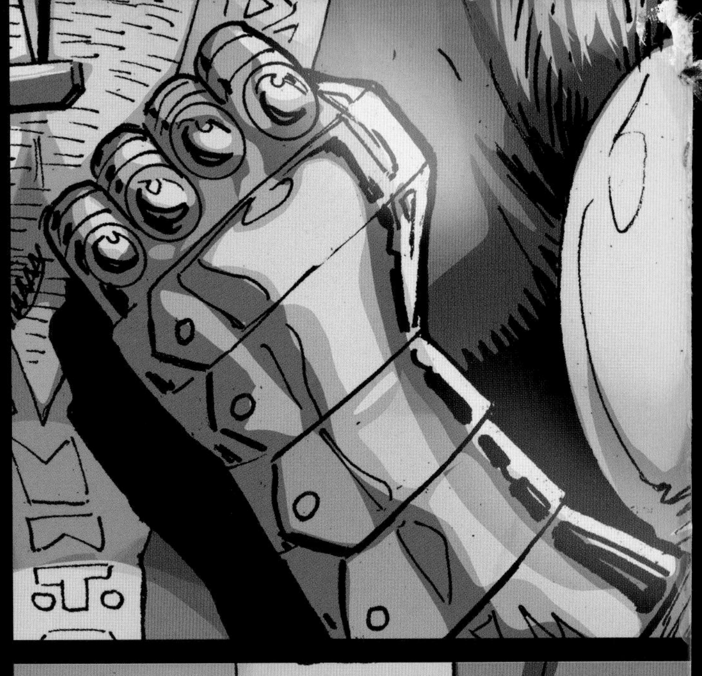

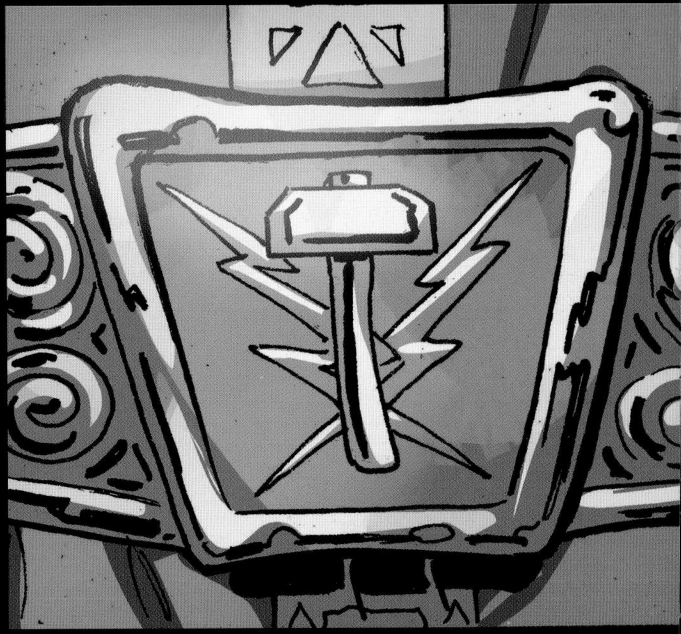

Printed in China.
010101S17

TABLE OF CONTENTS

LONG AGO...

The ancient Norse people lived in a cold, harsh world. Making their home in what we now call Scandinavia, they survived through farming, hunting, fishing, trading... and raiding. The Norse were skilled sailors and boat makers. Their warriors, fearless fighters known as Vikings, used the swift boats to set sail and pillage neighboring lands for essential supplies, or sometimes just for the glory of it. They were fierce people. And the gods they worshipped were even fiercer.

These gods were called the Aesir. Norse people believed their deities lived in the heavenly realm of Asgard and ruled over the Nine Worlds—the home of mortals, dwarves, elves, giants, and monsters. The gods were often beautiful, wise, and strong. But they could also be vain, weak, jealous, and foolish. Just like humans.

There was Odin, the wise and ruthless ruler of the Aesir. Thor, the proud and mighty thunder god. Loki, the sly shape-shifter who was born a giant but raised among the gods. Baldur, the pure and beloved god of light. Frigg, the powerful sorceress and queen of the Aesir. And many more gods and goddesses who dwelled in the halls of Asgard.

The Norse also believed terrible monsters walked through their world. Giants were chief among theses creatures. Huge and powerful, giants came from a harsh, mountainous land called Jötunheim. They often warred against the gods and threatened the lives of humans.

For hundreds of years, the Norse told tales of the Aesir and giants. Some have been lost over the ages and forgotten, but some still survive through ancient writings and epic poems. This book is a collection of four surviving stories: a tale of sibling rivalry, tales of battle and trickery, a tale of the death, and a tale of the end of the world—and it's new beginning.

So settle in and prepare yourself for adventure. Enter the world of old Norse myths.

THOR AND LOKI

Retelling by Carl Bowen
Pencils by Tod Smith
Colors by Rex Lokus

LOKI
THIALFI

Wrapped around its trunk lay Midgard.
It was our world—and yours.
Today, you might think
of it as the "real" world.
Below Yggdrasil's roots lay Niflheim,
the icy home of the dishonored dead.
Opposite it lay Muspelheim,
the home of the fire giants.

At the top, among Yggdrasil's branches, lay Asgard.
It was the home of our gods, the Aesir.
Their ruler was one-eyed Odin, the All-Father. He was wise and cunning.
He was the greatest of the gods—or the worst, depending on whom you asked.

Thor, what brings you before me today? I have much to do.
All-Father, I've grown bored.
Bored, he said?
A bored Thor is a *troublesome* Thor.
What are your intentions then, son?
I wish to go into Jötunheim, the giants' land, with my hammer, *Mjölnir*.
I want to remind them why they should fear and respect us.

We have a peace treaty with the giants, son.
I will not break it. I just want to have a little fun.
Thor's idea of fun is *dangerous.*
He's like his brother Loki in that way.
Yes, those two require much looking after.
It must be hard to keep an eye on them both...
Yes...but perhaps they can do so together.

Thor was not pleased by his father's wishes. But he was an obedient and respectful son, so he did as he was told.

Loki was not Thor's brother by blood. In fact, Loki was not one of the gods at all. He was born a giant.

Odin had agreed to raise Loki along with his other sons. The resulting treaty brought peace between Asgard and Jötunheim.

But Thor had never trusted Loki. Nor had Thor's wife, Sif…

Sif, I only want to be friends.

Friends? When we were children, you once cut off all my hair as a cruel joke.

That was so long ago! I'd forgotten all about it.

My request is small. I just want to know where Thor keeps Mjölnir when he–
Sif? Are you here?
Hello, husband!

My love, I'm off to Jötunheim for a while. Have you seen Loki?
He's here. We were just talking about you.
Brother, I'm off to Jötunheim.
Yes, so you said.
Odin says you must come with me.
Fine. As the All-Father wishes.

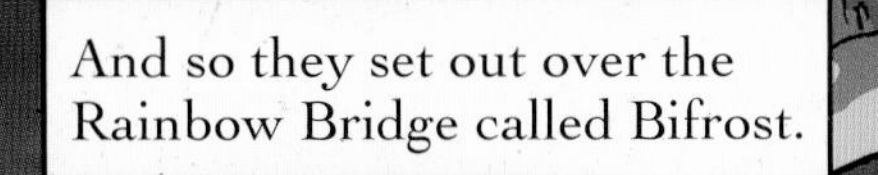

They rode in Thor's chariot, pulled by the magical goats Toothgnasher and Toothgrinder.

CHAPTER 2
AN UNFORTUNATE DEED
At the end of the first day, they came to the home of the mortal Egil and stopped to rest.
Your visit honors me, noble guests...but I'm afraid I have no food fit for gods.
Too bad.
Don't worry about that, friend. I have just the thing...
Thor returned to his chariot...
...and killed his two goats.
CRACK

Thor cooked the goats for Loki and himself, as well as Egil and his family.
They feasted well that night—except for Egil's son, Thialfi.
After eating, Thor lay the goats' bones aside and covered them with their skins.
See that these aren't touched. It's very *important*.
Thialfi was shocked by the events of the night. And who wouldn't be?
Hmm...

Would you like to know a secret, boy? Thor's goats are *magical* creatures. Tomorrow they will rise from the dead.

Really?

Oh yes.

We eat them all the time, Thor and I. I've heard that the best part is the *marrow* in their bones. Though I've never tried it myself...

magic to trick a
curious boy...
SNAP!
The next morning, Thor tried
to use Mjölnir's magic to bring
his goats back to life.
But when he did...
...the bone that Thialfi
had broken was not
made whole.

Thor was furious. Frightened, Thialfi confessed to the deed.
Do you have any idea what you've *done*?!
Egil begged Thor for forgiveness. He even offered to give his son to Thor as a servant.
Fortunately for Thialfi, Thor accepted his father's offer.
Unfortunately for the goat, it would be lame for all its days.
Loki was pleased.

The three travelers set out on foot for Jötunheim later that morning. A long journey lay before them.
By nightfall, they had become lost in a deep forest.
We'll never reach Jötunheim at this rate. We should stop for the night.
I'll find us some shelter.
After some searching, Thialfi discovered a cave.
It's a little *musty* inside, but it should do.

CHAPTER 3
A GIANT AWAKENS
They settled in for the night. Hungry and tired, all they could do was try to go to sleep.
No sooner had they laid down…
RUMBLE RUMBLE
RUMBLE RUMBLE
RUMBLE RUMBLE
What in the Nine Worlds is that?
RUMBLE RUMBLE
RUMBLE RUMBLE

RUMBLE RUMBLE RUMBLE RUMBLE

Someone should go find out.

RUMBLE RUMBLE RUMBLE RUMBLE

Oh, very well.

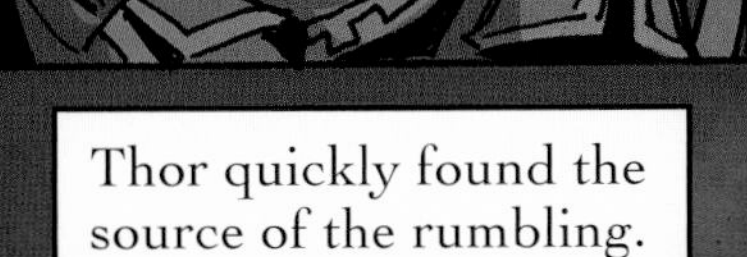

Thor quickly found the source of the rumbling.

SNORE SNORE

RUMBLE RUMBLE RUMBLE RUMBLE

SNORE SNORE

The largest giant he had ever seen was sleeping on the forest like it was a bed of straw.

RUMBLE RUMBLE

Thor returned to the cave.
as the *sky!*
What should we do?
Thor should go out there and smash its head in. It's what he's good at.
But he's sleeping!
Would you rather he woke up and stepped on all of us?
No.
Then get to it. Unless, of course, you're too *afraid.*

Thor is no coward!
I will!
Show us then.
After Thor had left...
Do you really believe Thor can defeat the giant?
Maybe, maybe not.
Either way I'll be happy.

Meanwhile…
BOOM!!

Hmm? What was that?
Did an acorn fall on my head?
Uh-oh.

Yaaaawnn...

Oh, hello there. Are you lost, little one?
I'm not lost. My name is Thor, son of Odin. I'm looking for Jötunheim.
I am Skrymir, and I'm looking for something as well...a *glove* I lost.
There it is!
The glove, Thor realized, was the very cave where he and the others had taken shelter!

What a relief. I thought I'd never find it.
Now, what were you saying?
Ooh... My back...
Jötunheim. M-my companions and I are going to Jötunheim.

Well, friend, the nearest city is Utgard, which is that way.
But beware the ruler of that place. He has powers you can't begin to imagine.
I fear no giant, Skrymir.
Good for you. Anyway, the sun is coming up. I should go.
I think we'll meet again soon, though. Farewell.

CHAPTER 4
CHALLENGES OF THE GIANT KING
As Skrymir walked away over the horizon, Thor and company set out as well.
You really taught *him!*
Be quiet.
By day's end, they arrived at Utgard, on the border of the giants' land.
It impressed them all.
However, the giants and their king, Utgarda-Loki, were less than impressed by them.

You are **not welcome** here. You may stay only if you have any special skills to show us.
This feels like a ***trick.***
No, this is why we came: to show how the sons of Asgard are better than any giant.
If that's ***really*** how you feel...

The first challenge Utgarda-Loki set was an eating contest.
Loki volunteered, boasting he could out-eat anyone. His opponent was named Logi.
With one great bite, Loki stripped all the meat from a leg of goat.
The giant, however, did him one better. He ate the entire thing—plus the plate.

Loki admitted defeat.
Utgarda-Loki's next test was a footrace against the giant Hugi.
Seeing the opponent, Thialfi volunteered.
I can beat this big *oaf!*
Go!
WOOSH
???

Finally, Thor claimed that he could out-drink any giant in Utgard. Utgarda-Loki smiled and handed Thor a drinking horn.
Let's see if you can finish *this.*
Thor took the horn and drank… and drank…and drank…
He drank for an hour straight, but he could not empty the horn.
Thor was forced to admit defeat.
So much for the *might* of the gods of Asgard!

I tire of these foolish contests! Let my *hammer* show you what we gods are made of!
Don't make me laugh. This *cat* sleeping by my fire is more intimidating than you.
If you could even lift it, I would be impressed.
You're not going to take that, are you?
Never!
Good man. Go lift that cat. Prove your worth.
Fool.

Struggle as he might, Thor could only lift one paw off the ground.
How impressive! You nearly lifted a single paw.
Perhaps there is one of my subjects you are worthy to fight...
To the giants' delight, their king sent for an old crone called Elli.
Stand against me if you can.
Brave Thor leapt into battle without a second thought.

Yet for all his fearsome strength, Thor found himself outmatched.

CHAPTER 5
A TRICKSTER REVEALED
The defeat was too much for the thunder god to endure...
Let's see how you laugh with your *teeth* knocked out!
Wait, brother! Things are not as they seem...
Tell him, Utgarda-Loki. Tell him the *truth.*
What truth?

Finally figured me out, have you? What gave it away?
The cat, of course.
I enjoy making a fool of Thor as much as any man, but that was far too silly to believe.
What's this about? I demand an explanation!
Our host is a skilled illusionist. He's been playing us all for fools.

So I have— from the moment you entered my forest!
That means Skrymir...
...was me.
Luckily, I thought to make myself look larger. Otherwise your hammer wouldn't have missed my head!
The challenges you've faced here were illusions as well. Let me show you.
Loki, you did well, but your opponent was really a roaring fire given the shape of a giant. No one, giant or god, could out-eat an inferno.

Thialfi, you are ***fleet of foot***, but your opponent was more cunning than you know.

Hugi was the speed of my mind given shape. You had no chance against my quick wit.

Thor, the drinking horn is magically linked to the bottom of the ***sea.*** It also changes the taste of saltwater to mead.

The illusion you wrestled against was no crone but ***Old Age*** itself, given form.

Eventually old age brings every one of us to our knees.

Ahh... the cat.
In truth, it was bound to a simple piece of rope running through a hole in the ground.
What's on the other end?
It loops around the neck of the *Midgard Serpent*...
"...Jörmungand!"
"What chance would any man—or god—have at lifting a beast coiled around the entire world?"

So I actually lifted the Midgard Serpent?!
Very slightly. An impressive display of strength, nonetheless.
You're right to fear the strength I've shown you, trickster!
For now it will make you pay for making fools of us!
FSSSSST

The king, his subjects, and their entire city disappeared!
Utgarda-Loki!!!
Where did it all go?
MIDGARD SERPENT DO NOT PULL
I think it was never really here. How clever.

Utgarda-Loki must have sent us the wrong way when he was disguised as Skrymir.
That's what I would have done.
You clearly share that villain's cunning, Loki. But tell me this...
...if you saw through his tricks when I lifted the cat, why not tell me right away?
Why let me wrestle that old woman? I looked like an idiot!
In any event, there's nothing more we can do here.
Yes. Let's go home. I'm tired of adventuring in the land of giants.

Retelling by Carl Bowen

Art by Eduardo Garcia

ODIN
FREYA
THOR
LOKI

GJALP
GREIP
GEIRRÖD

CHAPTER 1
GODS AND GIANTS
In the days of old, Jötunheim was a land of bitter cold and shrieking wind.
It lay across the river Ifing.
Giants lived there.
Despite their size, the giants were not so different from us. Some were good, kind folk, just like we gods of Asgard.
But stories of good, kind folk do not interest me.
I am Odin, All-Father of the gods. In all my years, I have known many giants.
And many of them were cruel, wicked creatures. Those stories are my favorites.

But those tales do not belong to the giants alone.
They also belong to my sons, Thor and Loki.
Loki himself was a giant, though a rather small one.
I took him in as a baby to help create peace between Asgard and Jötunheim ...between the gods and the giants.
Loki often gave me cause to regret raising him as one of my own.
Thor, on the other hand, was strong, brave, and tough.
He taught the giants to fear Asgard. To fear us.
My sons are gone now. I miss them terribly.
But they will live forever in their stories...

CHAPTER 2
THE TALE OF GEIRRÖD AND HIS DAUGHTERS
One day, Loki borrowed a magical cloak of falcon feathers from the lovely goddess Freya. The cloak turned anyone who wore it into a falcon.
Alone, Loki flew to visit Jötunheim, the land of the giants.
But once he crossed the river Ifing, Loki was spotted. A wicked giant called Geirröd saw through his disguise.
That falcon is not a falcon at all.

With a pair of tongs, Geirröd hurled a burning coal at Loki.
FSSZZZH
The coal singed Loki's cloak. Its magical spell was broken.
Agh!
Loki tumbled from the sky like a falling star.
WHUMP

When Loki landed, he found Geirröd and his daughters waiting.
You sly traitor to giants! Why have you come here?
Pin him to the earth like a bug, father!
No, let's lock him in a casket and bury him like the worm he is.
Perhaps we will do both.
Loki trembled at the threat. His bravery deserted him, but not his wit and cunning…
Wait! If you let me live, then I will give you Thor!

Yes. I can bring him here. Kill him, and the power of Asgard will be broken.
You would trade Thor's life for your own?
Very well. Bring him to me. But make sure he leaves his hammer, *Mjölnir*, at home.
Loki gave Geirröd his word. Then he returned home to Asgard.

Loki found Thor at his hall, Bilskirnir. In those days, Thor still trusted Loki.
Brother! I've just returned from *Jötunheim!*
I met two *beautiful* giant women named Gjalp and Greip. I told them all about you.
Go on...
They want to meet the mighty *Thor!* Are you interested?
Absolutely! We shall leave at once.

The brothers set out from Asgard in Thor's chariot.

They crossed Bifrost, the Rainbow Bridge, into Jötunheim.

At nightfall, Thor and Loki stopped to rest at the home of Grid.

Grid was a friendly giant. She welcomed them happily.

After dinner, while Loki slept, Thor told Grid why he was in Jötunheim.
I know Gjalp and Greip's father, Geirröd. He is a wicked giant.
He hates Asgard and all its gods. If you even *look* at his daughters, he will kill you.
And where is your hammer, Mjölnir?
My brother convinced me to leave it at home...
Hmm... wait here.

Where are those...a-ha! These should help.
This staff is magical. It is also unbreakable.
These gloves are as hard as iron and as flexible as leather.

Thank you, Grid. I'm certain these gifts will be useful.

The next morning, Thor and Loki set out once more.
Why didn't I get any gifts?
You snore.
Soon, they came to a river. The water was swift and cold.
They had to leave Thor's chariot behind.
These giant women had better be truly beautiful, Loki.
You won't believe your eyes, my brother. I promise.

Many hours later…
This is their home.
What if Geirröd is here? Grid warned me that he's an enemy of Asgard.
Are you afraid of a giant?
I thought the mighty Thor was braver than that.
Besides, Geirröd told me he'd be thrilled to have *Thor*, son of *Odin*, marry one of his daughters! Now get moving.
Ha! All right, brother. I'm going.

The house was dark and empty with only a single stool for furniture.
Go on inside, brother.
WELCOME, THOR... SIT, PLEASE...
Gjalp? Greip? Is that you? Don't be so shy!
PLEASE SIT DOWN. WE'LL COME OUT IN A MOMENT...
Ladies are so silly. Very well, I'll wait here.
As soon as Thor sat down ...

Gjalp and Greip emerged from their hiding place.

WOOSH

They grabbed the stool and tried to crush Thor against the roof beams overhead.

Outside, Loki assumed his treachery was complete . . .
Sorry, brother. It was you or me.
. . . but Thor still lived. He had crushed Gjalp and Greip in their own trap.
Sorry, girls. It was you or me.
With his daughters' trap foiled, Geirröd took matters into his own hands.
You will *die* for this, Asgardian!

Enraged by the death of his daughters, Geirröd hurled a flaming coal at Thor's head.
FWOOOOSH
SMACK
But Thor caught the deadly missile in his iron glove and ...
THONK
Ha! So much for giant *strength.*

Thor! You're alive?!
I take it that their father was home?
So he was. This whole meeting was a trap.
Wait, dear brother! Please, let me explain!
Yes, this was a trap— but not for you...

...IT WAS A TRAP FOR THEM!
You see, I knew you could handle them! That's why I took you to Grid's home first.
She gave you exactly what you needed to survive, remember?
Aye... that she did.
Because you're my brother, I choose to believe you, Loki.
But next time, please tell me the plan first.
Of course.
And so the brothers returned to Asgard, leaving the house of Geirröd behind forever.

CHAPTER 3

THE TALE OF THE CLAY GIANT

Some giants became our enemies not out of wickedness, but from stupidity. Hrungnir was one such giant.

As the ruler of Asgard, I once invited him for a meal. He was a poor guest.

He drank too much during dinner. Then he insulted me—and my wife, Frigg.

This little old man doesn't *deserve* a queen like you. You should marry me!

Unhand me, you Asgardian thug!
Quiet you!
And don't come back!
WHUMP
I will be back with my weapons! Then you'll regret treating a guest this way.
I look forward to it!

The very next morning ...
WHISPER WHISPER
...my raven told me Hrungnir was on his way back.
That foolish lout!
He carried a sturdy stone in one hand as a throwing weapon.
In his other hand, he held an unbreakable magic shield.
Mighty weapons indeed ...

…but before him strode his true weapon—a monster made of clay.
Hrungnir had created it with his magic.
He called it Mokkurkalfi.

The colossal monster shook the land with each step.
I sent Thor and his servant, Thialfi, to deal with Hrungnir and his creation.
Thor wore his magical iron gloves. A belt of giant strength circled his waist.
And in his hand, he held his mighty hammer, Mjölnir.
Hrungnir's shield is going to make things difficult for you.
Aye.
I have a plan. You greet the clay giant. I will take care of its master.
Aye.

While Thor waited for Mokkurkalfi, Thialfi dodged around the clay monster to face Hrungnir.
At the walls of Asgard, Thor greeted the gigantic clay monster...
That's *far enough*, monster!
...with a single blow.
THOK

With Mokkurkalfi easily defeated, Thor set out for Hrungnir.
Thialfi found the giant first.
Thor has defeated your clay giant, Hrungnir.
If you don't turn back, you will be next.
Ha! Even Mjölnir is no match for my shield, boy!
Thor knows this very well. That's why he won't attack you head on.
Instead, he's digging through the earth to attack you from below!
Oh yeah? Well let's see him dig through that!
Hrungnir, as I mentioned, was quite stupid.

When Thor arrived, Hrungnir saw that he'd been tricked.
He hurled his stone weapon at Thor's head.
But Thor hurled Mjölnir at the same time.
CRACK
It shattered the stone in midair ...
...and killed Hrungnir instantly.
THUD
What happened to the clay giant, Thor?
It should be here by now...
Aah!
About time.
BOOM

CHAPTER 4
THE TALE OF THE BRIDE OF THRYM
Elsewhere in Jötunheim lived a giant king named Thrym.
He was not hateful like Geirröd, nor stupid like Hrungnir.
No, Thrym was devious. Thrym was clever…
One night, he crept into Asgard in secret, right to Thor's home.
He stole Thor's magic hammer, Mjölnir, as the god slept.
The next morning…
Robbery!
Brother, what is it?
Mjölnir is gone! Stolen in the night!

Perhaps you just misplaced it?
I did not. Look—the thief's tracks are right outside my window.
So they are. And they're giant-sized. I bet they lead into Jötunheim.
Then that's where I'm going!
No, brother. This could be a trap. I have a better idea...

Loki first visited Freya in her hall, Sessrumnir, to ask for her help.
Why should I care?
Thor's hammer is Asgard's greatest weapon. He needs it back.

Without it, we're all at risk!
Fine. You can borrow my falcon cloak to look for it. It's over there.
Just be more *careful* with it this time.
Of course! You can trust me.

Loki soared over Asgard, following the thief's tracks.
The trail took him across the river Ifing, deep into the giants' land.
At last it led to the heart of Jötunheim: Thrym's castle.

Ho, Thrym! A fine day for a long flight, eh?
Skip the chit-chat, Loki. I know why you're here.

You want Thor's hammer back, don't you?
Yes, thanks. Do you have it here, or shall I wait for you to go get it?

I'll gladly give it back. But I want something first.
Bring me the goddess Freya. I wish to *marry* her.

Great.

Loki returned to Freya with Thrym's demand...
Absolutely not!
Freya, please reconsider.
Loki, I'm *already* married.
So what?
SLAP
Well... I tried.

Loki had no choice but to tell the rest of us what had happened.
We held a meeting in my own hall, Valaskjalf, to discuss it.
That is his demand. He'll only return the hammer if Freya marries him.

Otherwise, Mjölnir is lost to us.

I'll tear his castle down with my *bare hands* and take it back myself!
No! I forbid you from starting another war with the giants.

Freya, will you not consent to this? For the safety of Asgard?
Never! Thor may marry Thrym if he wants that hammer back so badly.
That's not a bad idea, actually...
May I suggest we *disguise* Thor as Freya?
That way, he can get close enough to the giant to get Mjölnir back.
I like no part of this plan except the end.
Oh, come now, brother. I would do the same for you.
No you wouldn't.

After much arguing and excuse making...
It's for the good of Asgard, after all.
Fine! Let's just get this over with.
Loki and Freya dressed Thor in a bridal gown and hid his face behind a veil.
I look *ridiculous*.
What does it matter how you look? It's what inside that counts.
Grrr...
We're ready, All-Father. What do you think?
I couldn't be happier. After all, every father dreams of the day his *daughter* goes off to be wed!
Grrr...

When the disguise was complete, we sent them off to Jötunheim.
They took Freya's chariot over the Rainbow Bridge, Bifrost.
Grrr...

Their journey was long but uneventful. Eventually, they arrived at Thrym's castle.
Finally.

They found all of Thrym's family gathered there. He had prepared a great feast.
Thrym greeted his new guests with great excitement. He invited them to join the party.

Thor and Loki took their seats at the giant's table.
Somehow, no one could tell that Thor was not the real Freya.
As Thor ate, however, Thrym grew suspicious.
Your appetite is...*impressive* for one so small.
OM NOM NOM

Lady Freya's journey was long, King Thrym, and she is excited to marry you.
Normally she's a light eater.

Convinced by Loki's lies, Thrym leaned over to kiss his bride-to-be.

What he saw when he peeked under Thor's veil, however, gave him pause.
Does the Lady Freya have a *beard?!*
Not at all! Freya is just... *dirty* from the long trip. She will bathe before her veil is removed at your wedding.
And if I may be so blunt, my king, you've also had a lot to drink tonight...
Oh... yes, perhaps you're right.
Thrym kept his hands (and lips) to himself after that.

When the meal was finished, and the kiss forgotten, Thrym stood up to address his guests.

Friends and family! We gather today not just for a feast—but for a wedding!

Today I make Asgard's loveliest... *woman*... my wife.

Of course. Someone bring Mjölnir to Loki so he may return it to Thor.

Look upon me, giants! Mjölnir is *mine*—and mine alone!
That's Thor...
...in a *dress*?
HAHAHAHAHA!
HAHAHAHAHA!

Consumed by his rage, Thor made the giants pay for their theft and mockery...

…there were no survivors.

When his fury was finally spent . . .
So much for the supposed *power* of giants.
Loki, where are you? I didn't kill you by accident, did I?
I'm...fine. How are you? Are you...feeling better?

I am weary. Weary of this plan, this dress, and this place.
Let's return to Asgard and be done with this nonsense.
Agreed!
Freya will not be happy with what I've done to her dress...
She'll get over it. She has nearly a thousand of them, after all.
You're a good brother, Loki.
Thank you, my brother.
You're welcome.

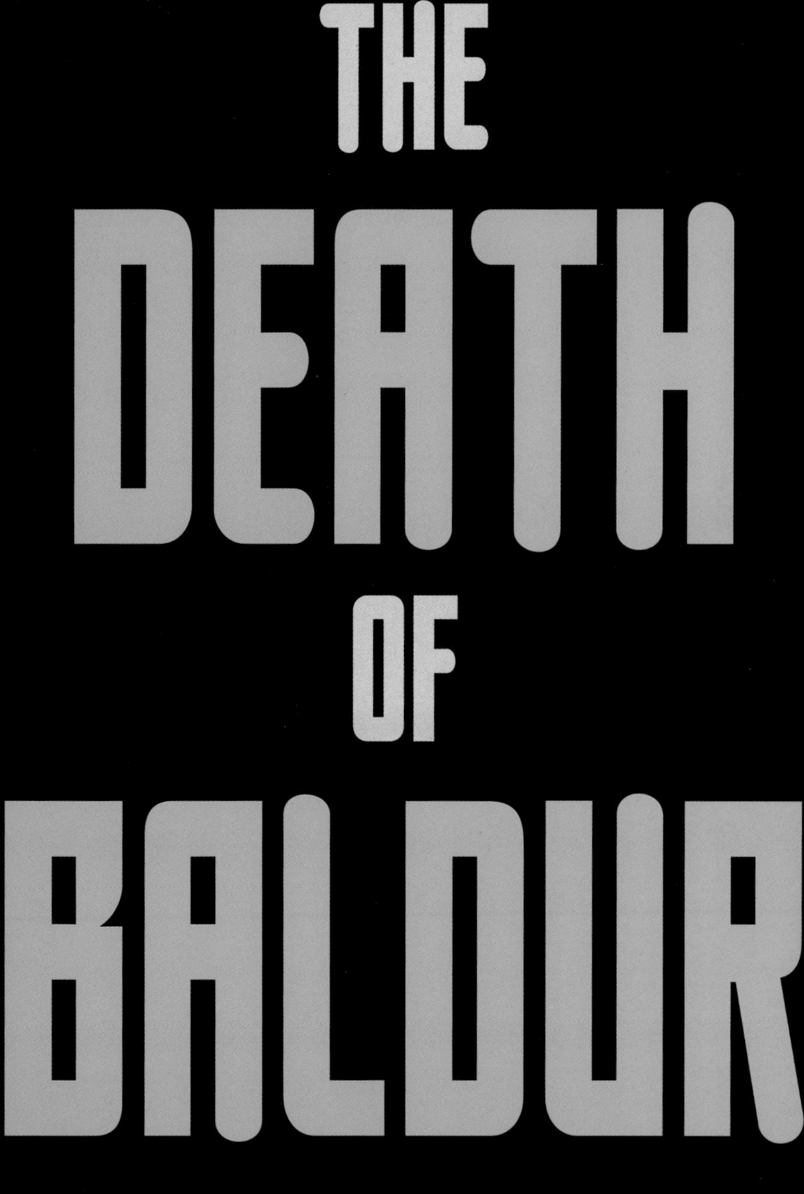

Retelling by Louise Simonson
Art by Eduardo Garcia

BALDUR
LOKI

THOR
ODIN

CHAPTER 1

DREAMS AND NIGHTMARES

He is the *favorite* of all who dwell in Asgard.
Odin's words were true. Everyone loved Baldur most, except for one person—Loki.
Loki was a giant born in the icy world of Jötunheim. He was taken in by Odin and raised among the gods of Asgard.

Loki often used his magical abilities to cause trouble. To make up for it, he gave the gods wondrous gifts…
Thor's hammer, Mjölnir.
Odin's spear, Gungnir.
Odin's eight-legged horse, Sleipnir.
I have made my share of trouble, but at least I *apologized!*
Loki had two wives, Sigyn and Angrboda. They had many children together. But Angrboda's children were monsters…
The great serpent, Jörmungand.
And the half-woman and half-monster, Hel.
The enormous wolf, Fenrir.

One day, a seer told Odin that Loki's children would play an important role in Ragnarök—the end of the world.
Therefore, Odin banished Hel to rule Niflheim, the land of the dead.
He had Fenrir chained.
And he cast Jörmungand into the sea.
Odin's acts delayed the Doom of the Gods...
...but they also angered Loki. And as the years went by, his rage only grew.

A few years later, Baldur married the goddess Nanna. Loki was not invited...
Baldur, my heart is glad to know you've found true love.
They lived happily in Baldur's palace, Breidablik.

In time, their son Forseti was born.
My grandson is *almost* as beautiful as his father!
Soon after, Baldur's nightmares began…
No! No…
…No!
Baldur, wake up!

I was attacked. Death came for me!
You were only dreaming, my husband.
It seemed so real.
Then you must tell Frigg. Surely the goddess of wisdom will know what to do!
It was just a bad dream. I don't want to worry my mother.
But night after night, the dreams returned. Baldur was forced to ask Frigg their meaning.
What do you think, Mother?
One nightmare is likely just that—a bad dream.

But when the same dream returns, again and again, it is a ***warning.***

But fear not, my son. I know what to do.

CHAPTER 2

A MOTHER'S PROTECTION

The task was nearly fatal, even for a goddess...but Frigg would do anything to protect her favorite son.

Frigg called upon everything in nature that could possibly hurt Baldur. She forced each and every one of them to promise that they would not harm her son.

From the largest dragon to the tiniest microbes, Frigg conjured all that could cause harm.

From metals to stone, wood and bone—anything from which weapons could be made.

They all loved the beautiful and gentle Baldur. And so, in turn, all of them swore to protect her son.

Baldur tested the promises that all things had made to Frigg.
Wolves would not attack him.
Even Thor's lightning would not strike him.
The sea itself lifted Baldur up to protect him from harm.

To be absolutely sure of Baldur's safety, the gods hurled everything they could find at him…
…for no weapon could hurt him.
Incredible!
Our brother is invulnerable!
Loki was not pleased.
There must be a way around Frigg's magic...

Perhaps my *own* magic will do the trick...
Fooling Frigg with flattery should be easy enough...

Queen of Asgard, you were so wise to find a way to protect Baldur!
Thank you, good woman. It wasn't easy to convince everything in the world to keep him safe.
Everything...?
Well...between you and me, there is a tiny plant called mistletoe that grows far to the west.
It is so **weak** and **small**, I didn't think it could possibly do any harm. I didn't bother to ask it for protection.
Ahh. Mistletoe.

Loki immediately rode west.
He found a cluster of mistletoe high up in the branches of a mighty oak.

He studied it carefully.

It is a parasite that feeds off the tree it lives on. Individually, its branches are small and weak...

SNAP

CHAPTER 3
DEATH OF A GOD
When Loki returned to the High Hall of Asgard, the gods were still hurling weapons at Baldur for amusement.
Well met, Hodur! This hall is filled with laughter. Why are you so glum?
I'm not glum, Loki. I'm simply bored. Being blind, I can't see the fun.
And even if I could see, I have nothing to throw at Baldur.

I can't cure your blindness, Hodur... but I *can* give you something to throw at your brother.

It's small, but it will let you join in the fun.

Here, let me help you aim...
Perfect. Now throw the dart with all your might!
FWOOSH!!

No...

When the dart found its mark, Odin knew the prophecy of the Doom of the Gods had been set in motion.

WHUMP
Baldur!
He's dead! My beloved husband is *dead!*
Whose weapon killed him?!

I threw it. But I didn't think it would hurt—
You have *murdered* the best of all of us!
You will *die* for your betrayal!
SHUCK
Ah!

A dart made of mistletoe has killed my son? I thought it too small and weak to cause harm...
Frigg tried to comfort Nanna...
...but she had died of a broken heart.
The realm of the dead has claimed them both!

Hermod, you are swift and sure. Ride Sleipnir into Niflheim.
Speak to Hel, who rules the underworld. In my name, ask her to let Baldur return to Asgard.
I will leave *immediately*, All-Father.

Chapter 4
Grief for the Dead

Brave Hermod soon reached Niflheim, but he had doubts that the plan would work.

Everyone in the world must shed a tear for Baldur's death. The dead and the living.
If even one refuses to weep, Baldur will remain in Niflheim with me.
The task would be nearly impossible. But Baldur was beloved by all, so no effort was spared.
It is Hel's demand, All-Father.
Make it so.

Again Frigg conjured all things. She asked them to weep for her son.
All things wept for Baldur.
Odin sent messengers far and wide to speak to everyone in all the worlds…
…and all who learned of Baldur's death wept.

Last of all, Hermod ventured to a cave in Jötunheim. There he found Thokk, the giantess.
I will not weep for Baldur. Odin's son means *nothing* to me!

I must tell the All-Father.

The gods dressed Baldur's body in his finest clothes. They carried him and Nanna to his ship, Ringhorn.

They were placed upon a funeral pyre.
Thor set the ship aflame with lightning from his hammer.
KRAKA BOOM
Finally, Hyrrokkin the giantess pushed the ship out to sea.

CHAPTER 5
CATCHING THE KILLER
To Baldur, who was taken from us too soon!
To Baldur!
On the seventh day after Baldur's death, as was their custom, the gods held a banquet in his honor.
Loki was not invited…
…but he couldn't resist the opportunity to gloat.
Thor is a better fighter than Baldur ever was. Hermod is the better rider.
Vali is braver! Silent Vidar's smarter. Even blind Hodur was more perceptive.
And compared to Odin, Baldur was a fool!
You should be glad he's dead! You should thank me!

Loki... you killed Baldur?!
I will *slay* him!
Run or *die*, Loki!

Loki ran.

He fled to a remote mountaintop.
How will I hide from the All-Father's sight during the day?

Of *course!*

Even *Odin* won't be looking for a fish!

Every night, Loki returned to his true form.
He sat by his fire, repairing the fishing net he used to catch his dinner.
Sigh.

After a while…
Surely they've stopped looking for me by now!
I long to see the *sun* again.

But Odin's patience was endless. And from his High Seat, he could see across all the Nine Worlds.
I have you now, Loki!

Go find Loki! He's beside a stream beyond the *farthest* mountaintop.

After many days...
Hoofbeats?
The gods are coming for me! I must *destroy* all evidence of being here.
SPLASH

This is the spot! That has to be Loki's fire...but where is he?

A fishing net!
Perhaps Loki has taken the *form* of that which he ate?

Let's mend the net and fish for shape-shifters.
Agreed.

Loki is clever. Catching him won't be easy.
And, indeed, it was not.
Never have I *seen* a *fish* so large! That must be Loki!
SPLOOSH!

Again Hermod threw the net.
Again, Loki evaded it.
He's heading for the *waterfall!*
A *third throw* of the net?

SWOOSH
You *fools* never learn. I cannot be caught.

WHAT... HOW?!

Now, Loki— you will pay for killing Baldur.

At Odin's command, the giantess Skadi led the gods to an icy cave on a high mountaintop.
Won't Loki try to change his shape to escape punishment?
Odin's magic has bound Loki. These *chains* will prevent him from his usual tricks.
This is a *fitting* prison!
And *this* is a fitting punishment.

The serpent's venom will drip onto Loki's face.
When he writhes in pain...
Aargh!
...the entire world will shudder with him!
This constant shaking can't be *safe!*
Do not worry. It is the will of the All-Father, and Odin knows all!

They left Loki to his fate.
Isn't that Loki's wife Sigyn? She might free him. Should we drive her away?
That is beyond her abilities.
All she can give Loki is comfort.
So Sigyn sat beside Loki and caught the venom in a bowl.
But whenever she left to empty it, Loki would writhe in pain…
GRAHHH!
GRAHHH!!!
…and all the Earth would tremble.

With Baldur's death, Odin knew the end of the world, Ragnarök, was at hand.

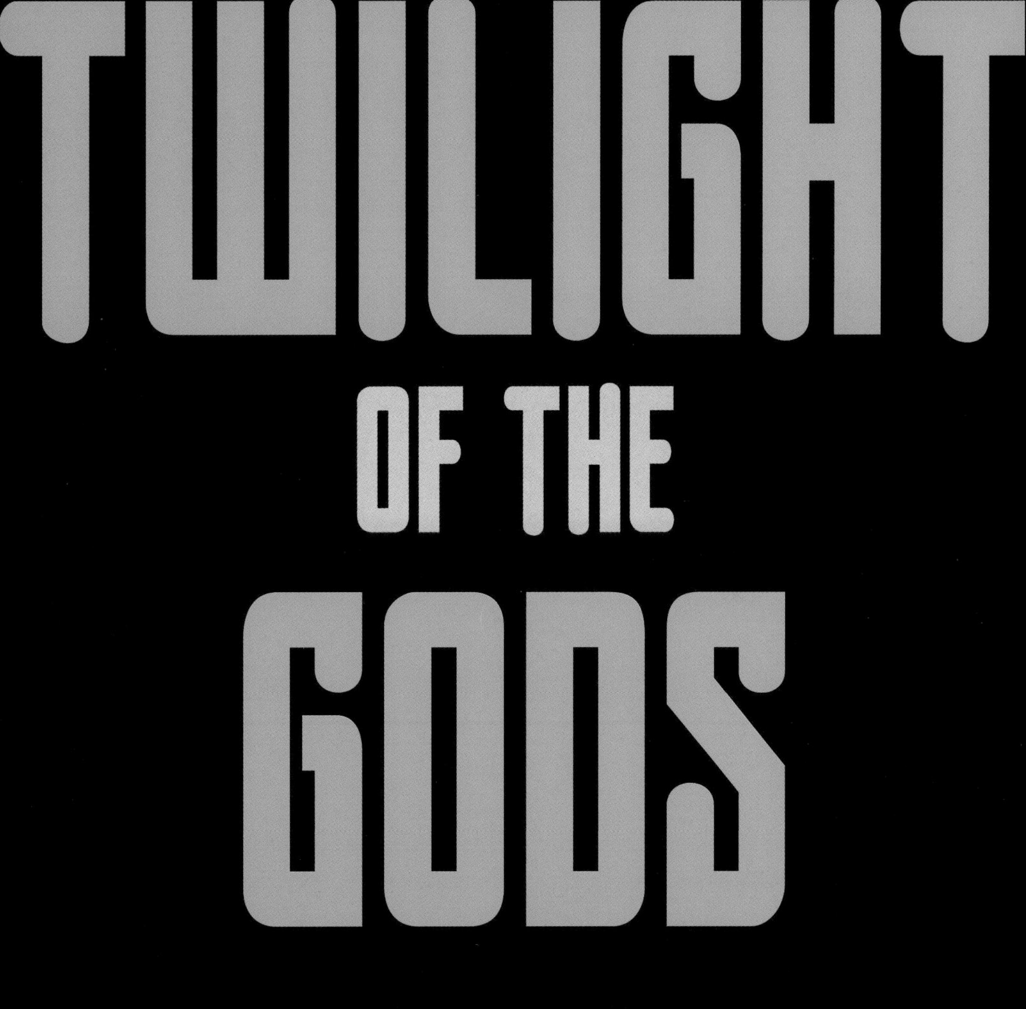

RETELLING BY MICHAEL DAHL
ART BY EDUARDO GARCIA

FREY
ODIN

SURT
THOR
LOKI

The gods of Asgard and the giants have long been at war with each other.
Odin, father of the gods, wanted peace with the giants. So he took in Loki, a young giant, and raised him among the other gods.
But Loki later betrayed the Aesir.

Loki was jealous of Baldur, Odin's favored son.
He created a dart of mistletoe and killed his adoptive brother.
In so doing, Loki set in motion the events that would lead to the end of the world…
TWILIGHT OF THE GODS

CHAPTER 1
THE BREAKING OF CHAINS

For his crime, Loki was imprisoned and punished…

None felt pity for Loki. He was a giant, after all, and they were gods from Asgard.
And Odin's decisions were *final*.
But after the gods left the scene...

Sigyn... my second wife.

Tssssssssssss
I bring comfort, my husband.

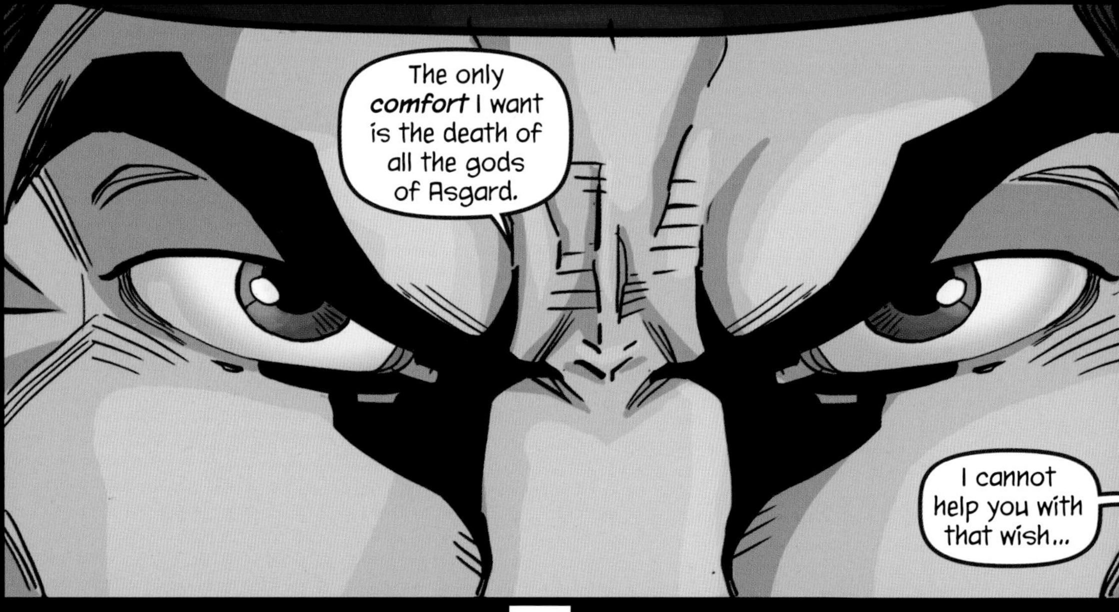
The only *comfort* I want is the death of all the gods of Asgard.
I cannot help you with that wish...

I know. That is why I must call on my first wife for her help.
Oh, Angrboda, hear me...!
Deep within a forest called the Iron Wood...
I hear you, my husband. What do you command?
...Release our children!

My children, your father calls. Your destiny calls...
DESTROY THE GODS!
The vicious wolves are Sköll, which is Treachery...
GRRRRR!

...and Hati, which is Hatred!
ROAARRR!
The two great wolves devour the sun and moon. With the lights of the heavens gone...

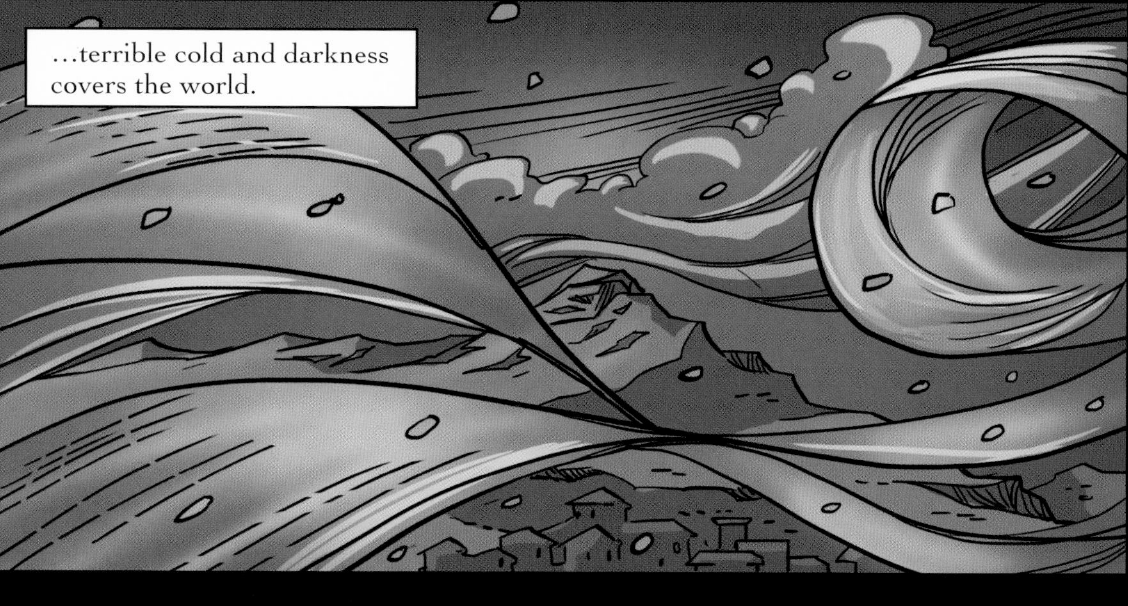
…terrible cold and darkness
covers the world.

On Bifrost, the bridge that stretches from the heavens to earth, stands Heimdall, the watchman of the gods.
Hail, mighty Thor!
Hail, Heimdall! Winter still rules the earth. Summer and spring have vanished.
Why do you frown, ever-watchful Heimdall?
I hear the sound of *death*, Thor.

Yggdrasil—the World Tree, which supports the worlds of gods and mortals with its mighty branches.
It is the sound of *dragon teeth!*

Nidhogg is devouring the *roots* of the World Tree...
And as Yggdrasil shakes, the *entire* universe trembles!

Meanwhile, back in Asgard, the realm of the gods...
I now hear the breaking of chains! Loki is free!
The shuddering of Yggdrasil has loosened Loki's bonds.
Freedom!
CLINK
CLINK
Husband, please don't go! You are heading to your doom!
Bah! I make my own fate.

I hear yet more chains breaking.
More enemies of the gods?
I fear so, yes. And more allies of the giants.
SNARL!
The chains of the great wolf, *Fenrir*, have also been shaken loose.
But most *terrible* of all...

...GARM, the guardian of the underworld, has also broken free!
ARRROOOOOO!
Garm is free? Then Ragnarök has truly arrived...
...The Twilight of the Gods is at hand.

Sound your *horn*, Heimdall! Call the gods of Asgard!
HARROOOOOOO
HARROOOOOOO

CHAPTER 2
THE GATHERING ARMIES
The Aesir gather at Heimdall's call.

Look, my brothers, the ocean rises.
This is the work of JÖRMUNGAND!

The monstrous serpent, the spawn of Loki, whips the waves of the ocean. The growing flood reaches the gates of Jötunheim, home of the giants.
Naglfar—a vessel made of dead men's fingernails. The ship was built by the giants through untold ages, waiting for this fated day.

Loki pilots the ship, leading the giants against the gods of Asgard.

Odin calls out to the god of strength and sunlight.
Frey! We need your ship!
Yes, All-Father!

Forward, champions of Asgard!
The Fates have given us this day. A day of *death* and *battle!*
If the gods are doomed to fall— then we shall take our *foes* with us!
Fight for *eternal glory!*

CHAPTER 3
THE WAR OF THE GODS
The Plain of Vigrid…the final battleground.
A third army arrives to join the battle.
Hel, queen of the underworld and ally to the giants, leads an army of the dead against the gods.
The great dog Garm hungers for blood…
GRRRRR!

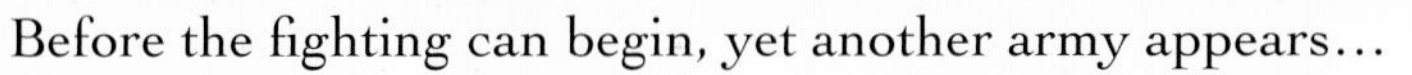
Before the fighting can begin, yet another army appears…

Look, my brother. It is our ancient foe, *Surt!* The demon has brought the fiery warriors of Muspelheim!
Doom to Odin! I shall bring death to the gods who *exiled* me to the edge of the world.

The forces prepare for battle, three armies against one. The giants, the dead, and the legions of fire—all against the Aesir!

As the armies face each other, another prophecy comes true. The last battle is announced by the screams of Hresvelgr, the Swallower of Corpses.

The End of All Things has begun!
For Asgard!
WHUMP

Amid the chaos of battle, Hel orders Garm to slay Tyr, the god of war.
Destroy him, my beauty!
Back to the underworld, you creature of darkness!
GRRRRR!

ROAR!
GRRRRR!

NO! Tyr has fallen!
Do you mourn your brother, Frey?
Then you can join him!
KRRSSSHH

You shall pay *dearly* for that!
FWSSSS
WOOOSH
Ha! You cannot harm me.
This day I have killed *both* beast and rider!
SHLICK

Meanwhile, Odin fends off the attacks of the ferocious Fenrir...
I don't care that Ragnarök is here. If I am to die, I'll take you with me, *foul beast!*

CRUNCH
...NOOO ASGARD...

CHAPTER 4
THE LAST STAND OF THE AESIR
On the other side of the world, in the Forest of Memory…
Vidar, the silent…the solitary…has long mourned his fallen brother, Baldur.
Vidar hears his father's dying cry on the wind.
ASGARD!
My father!

I come—
for you...
...and for
Asgard!
GRRRRR!

My *father* will be *avenged!*

CRUNCH!!

I couldn't save you, father. But your killer will never kill again.

Across the plain of battle, Heimdall and Loki meet…
Your king has fallen, Heimdall. After I defeat you, I shall destroy my so-called brother Thor!
Never!
I can hear the beating of your heart, evil one. Is it *fear* that grips you?
CLINK
You are mistaken, Heimdall...
What you hear is the sound of *triumph!*
SHLICK

You won't win this day, *traitor!*
NOOOO!
Above the battlefield, something terrible approaches…
By the *sword* of Odin!

Jörmungand! The Midgard Serpent!
I have fought you once before. This time I will destroy you!

Behold the *power* of Mjölnir!
KRAAKKK BOOM

KABOOM

My hammer and hand have won the *victory!*

No enemy blade or spear could fell the mighty Thor. Only the poisonous breath of evil.

Surt smiles with victory. His burning sword glows brighter...
...the Twilight of the Gods is at hand.

Ragnarök—the end of the world—has come.

CHAPTER 5

A NEW WORLD

The flames consumed all, leaving behind only darkness. Complete emptiness touched every corner of the world...

He will soon become the leader of the new gods.

Everything must come to an ***end...***

...but with every ending, comes a ***new beginning!***

GODS, MONSTERS, AND MORE:

A NORSE MYTHS GLOSSARY

AESIR (AY-zir)—The name given to the collection of gods and goddesses found in the ancient Norse religion. The Aesir live in Asgard, home of the gods, under the rule of the wise chief god, Odin.

ANGRBODA (AHN-goor-boh-da)—A giantess and one of the wives of the trickster Loki. Angrboda has three children: Fenrir, the giant wolf; Jörmungand, the huge serpent; and Hel, the goddess of death. The Aesir abducted and locked away Angrboda's offspring after the chief god, Odin, discovered they would play an important role at Ragnarök, the end of the world.

ASGARD (AHS-gahrd)—The home of the Aesir gods and one of the Nine Worlds. Asgard sits among the branches of the great World Tree, Yggdrasil.

BALDUR (BAWL-doorr)—The handsome god of light and most beloved son of the chief god, Odin, and his wife, Frigg. Baldur is so good and pure that all creatures and people throughout the Nine Worlds adore him. After Baldur starts having horrible nightmares that seem to foretell his death, Frigg uses her sorcery to protect him. She makes everything in the worlds vow not to harm him—everything except mistletoe, a plant so small it's thought to be harmless.

BIFROST (BAHY-frawst)—The bridge that connects Asgard, the world of the gods, to Midgard, the world of humans. The gods constructed it out of fire, air, and water, and it is incredibly sturdy. Also called the Rainbow Bridge, from Midgard the bridge appears as a rainbow that stretches from the earth to the sky. The god Heimdall vigilantly guards Bifrost to prevent giants and other intruders from entering Asgard.

BILSKIRNIR (BIL-skeer-neer)—The hall of the god Thor, located in Asgard. It is one of the largest buildings in Asgard with 540 rooms—fitting of a god who loves large feasts and celebrations.

BREIDABLIK (BRAY-da-blik)—The beautiful hall of the god Baldur, located in Asgard. Nothing impure is allowed to enter the hallowed building.

ELLI (EL-ee)—Old age in the form of an elderly giantess. In the hall of the giant king Utgarda-Loki, Thor is tricked into wrestling Elli. Thor believes she's just an old woman and can easily be beaten, but no one can defeat old age.

FENRIR (FEN-rir)—The enormous wolf and son of the trickster Loki and the giantess Angrboda. Fenrir's siblings are Jörmungand, the huge serpent, and Hel, goddess of death. Fenrir is so large that when he opens his mouth, his jaws stretch from the earth to the sky. The gods feared the wolf, so they tricked Fenrir into being tied up with special unbreakable chains crafted by dwarves. He remains bound until Ragnarök, the end of the world. During that time, Fenrir is destined to break free of his chains.

FORSETI (FOHR-set-ee)—The god of justice and son of the god Baldur and the goddess Nanna.

FREY (FRAY)—The god of the sun, rain, and harvest and brother of the goddess Freya. Frey has many magical treasures, including the ship Skidbladnir. Skidbladnir is large enough to hold all the Aesir, but it can be folded down small enough to carry in a pouch. When Frey rides into battle, he sits atop a large golden boar called Gullinborsti.

FREYA (FRAY-uh)—The goddess of love and fertility and sister of the god Frey. Freya is the most beautiful of all the goddesses. Gods, giants, and dwarves frequently fall in love with her—even though she is married to a mysterious god called Od. Freya owns a cloak of falcon feathers that grants the wearer the ability to fly, but she often rides in a chariot pulled by two cats instead. Although Freya is the goddess of love, she is also associated with battle. Souls of dead warriors are welcome in her hall, Sessrumnir.

FRIGG (FRIG)—The queen of the Aesir and wife of Odin. Frigg is the goddess of love, marriage, and motherhood. But Frigg is also a wise seeress and magician. It is said she knows the fate of every person but never reveals it. Her sons include Baldur, Hodur, and Hermod.

GARM (GAHRM)—A monstrous, howling dog that guards the gates of the underworld. At Ragnarök, the end of the world, Garm leaves the realm of the dead to battle the Aesir.

GEIRRÖD (GAY-rohd)—A nasty giant from the land of Jötunheim. Known as the Spear-Reddener, Geirröd hates the Aesir and longs to tear down the halls of Asgard. He has two daughters, Gjalp and Greip, who share his loathing. Together, the family plots to kill the mighty thunder god, Thor.

GIANTS—Towering and terrifying creatures who often war against the Aesir and humans. Giants mainly live in Jötunheim, one of the Nine Worlds. There are several kinds of giants: frost giants, fire giants, and rock giants. Although many giants hate the gods, not all of them hunger for battle. Some giants are friendly, helping the gods on their adventures or even marrying and having children with them. But at Ragnarök, the end of the world, giants and gods engage in an epic and bloody battle that leaves few survivors.

GIMLI (GIM-leh)—A shining, glittering palace and the tallest structure in Asgard. Gimli is said to be more beautiful than the sun and roofed in gold. It is the only palace that still stands after the final battle at Ragnarök.

GJALLARHORN (YAHL-ahr-hawrn)—The trumpet horn of Heimdall, the watchman of the gods. At Ragnarök, the end of the world, the horn sounds throughout the Nine Worlds, summoning all gods and warriors to the final battle.

GJALP (GEE-yalp) and **GREIP** (GRAYP)—The daughters of the brutal giant Geirröd. Like their father, the giantess sisters live to see the people of Asgard humbled and killed. They plot to kill the mighty thunder god, Thor.

GRID (GRID)—A friendly giantess. Grid is an ally of the Aesir and helps Thor on his journey to the home of the evil giant Geirröd.

GUNGNIR (GUNG-neer)—The magic spear that never misses its mark and belongs to the chief god, Odin. The weapon was crafted by dwarves and given to Odin by Loki.

HATI (HAW-tee)—A giant wolf that devours the moon at Ragnarök, the final battle. A second wolf, Sköll, eats the sun.

Heimdall (HAYM-dahl)—The watchman of the gods who guards Bifrost. With his sharp senses, Heimdall can see for one hundred miles in every direction and can hear the grass growing. Heimdall sounds his horn, Gjallarhorn, to call the Aesir and warriors to the final battle at Ragnarök.

Hel (HEL)—The half-human, half-monster goddess of death and ruler of the underworld. Hel is the daughter of the trickster Loki and the giantess Angrboda. Her brothers are Jörmungand, the huge serpent, and Fenrir, the giant wolf. The chief god, Odin, banished Hel to rule bitter cold Niflheim, one of the Nine Worlds, because she will play a part in the final battle at Ragnarök.

Hermod (HAIR-mohd)—The messenger of the gods and loyal son of the chief god, Odin, and the goddess Frigg. Hermod makes the treacherous journey into the underworld to ask Hel to release his brother Baldur.

High Seat—Odin's throne in Asgard. From the High Seat, Odin can observe all that happens in the Nine Worlds.

Hodur (HAW-doorr)—The blind god of winter and darkness, and son of the chief god, Odin, and the goddess Frigg. He is unable to participate in the Aesir's games and is easily deceived.

Hrungnir (HROONG-neer)—A large giant who is known for being among the strongest of his kind. He also commands a fearsome clay giant called Mokkurkalfi. However, Hrungnir is stone-headed. He foolishly challenges the mighty god Thor to battle.

Hugi (HOO-yee)—Thought in the form of a large giant. In the hall of the giant king Utgarda-Loki, the speedy Thialfi, Thor's human servant, is tricked into racing Hugi. But nothing can move faster than thought.

Hyrrokkin (HAY-roh-keen)—The giantess who pushes Baldur's ship, which was serving as the light god's funeral pyre, out to sea.

Ifing (EE-fing)—The coursing river that separates Asgard, the world of the gods, and the Jötunheim, the world of the giants.

Iron Wood—The forest east of Midgard where a wicked giantess lives. There, she raises her wolf children, including the monstrous wolves Sköll and Hati who devour the sun and moon at Ragnarök, the final battle.

Jörmungand (YOHR-moon-gahnd)—The huge snake, also known as the Midgard Serpent or World Serpent, and son of the trickster Loki and the giantess Angrboda. His siblings are Fenrir, the giant wolf, and Hel, the goddess of death. The chief god, Odin, cast Jörmungand into the sea, where he is doomed to circle Midgard with his tail clamped in his mouth. The serpent and the god Thor are great enemies, and the two meet at Ragnarök for one final battle.

Jötunheim (YOH-toon-haym)—The land of the giants. One of the Nine Worlds, Jötunheim is a harsh, freezing, mountainous place.

Logi (LOR-gee)—A roaring fire in the form of a young giant. In the hall of the giant king Utgarda-Loki, the trickster Loki is misled into an eating contest with Logi. But fire quickly consumes anything and everything, so Loki is bound to lose.

Loki (LOH-kee)—A trickster and cunning shape-shifter, Loki is both friend and foe to the Aesir. Born a small giant, Loki was taken in and raised by Odin, the chief god, in order to make peace with the giants. But Loki does not always get along well with his adopted family. He enjoys playing tricks and causing trouble however he can. Although Loki helps the Aesir when it suits his purpose, he ultimately stands against them at Ragnarök, the final battle. Loki is married to the giantess Angrboda and to the goddess Sigyn. He has three children with Angrboda: Fenrir, the giant wolf; Jörmungand, the huge serpent; and Hel, the goddess of death. His children also play an important part in the end of days.

Midgard (MID-gahrd)—The land of humans, also called Middle Earth. One of the Nine Worlds, Midgard is located around the trunk of Yggdrasil, the World Tree. It lies midway between Asgard, home of the gods, and Jötunheim, home of the giants.

Mjölnir (MYOHL-neer)—The hammer of the god Thor. A mighty weapon, Mjölnir always hits its mark and always returns to Thor's hand. It even shrinks in size to fit inside the thunder god's tunic. With Mjölnir, Thor can easily slay giants and protect Asgard from its enemies.

MOKKURKALFI (moh-koor-KAL-fee)—A huge clay monster created by the giant Hrungnir. Mokkurkalfi towers nine leagues tall and three leagues wide.

MUSPELHEIM (MOO-spel-haym)—A fiery, harsh land. One of the Nine Worlds, Muspelheim lies below the roots of Yggdrasil, the World Tree, and next to Niflheim, the land of bitter cold and perpetual darkness.

NAGLFAR (NAHGL-far)—The ship slowly built by giants through the ages and crafted out of dead men's fingernails. It carries the enemies of the Aesir to the final battle at Ragnarök.

NANNA (NAH-nah)—A goddess and the wife of the doomed god Baldur. She dies from grief at her beloved husband's untimely death and accompanies him to the land of the dead.

NIDHOGG (NEED-hawg)—The dragon that dwells in Niflheim, the bitter cold home of the underworld. Nidhogg constantly gnaws on the roots of the Yggdrasil, the World Tree. The beast also feeds on corpses that enter the realm of the dead.

NIFLHEIM (NIF-uhl-haym)—The icy home of the underworld that is ruled by Hel, the goddess of the dead. It is a vast wasteland filled with endless night and freezing fog. One of the Nine Worlds, Niflheim sits below the roots of Yggdrasil, the World Tree. Next to it lays Muspelheim, the land of fire.

NINE WORLDS—The nine worlds in Norse mythology, connected and bound by Yggdrasil, the World Tree. The Nine Worlds are often broken up into three levels. At the top is Asgard, home of the gods; Vanaheim, home of old gods called the Vanir; and Alfheim, home of the light elves. At the middle level is Midgard, home of humans; Jötunheim, home of the giants; Svartalfheim, home of the dark elves; and Nidavellir, home of the dwarves. At the bottom level is Niflheim, the frozen home of the dead, and Muspelheim, the land of fire.

NORSE—The ancient people who lived in Scandinavia, a region in northwest Europe that includes modern day Denmark, Norway, and Sweden, and usually Finland and Iceland. Much of Norse mythology—the stories and beliefs about gods, creation, and end of the world—comes from poems written down late in the Middle Ages, although the tales and worship of Norse gods started long before.

ODIN (OH-din)—The ruler of the Aesir. Also called the All-Father, Odin is one of the most ancient gods. He is the god of war and death, but also the god of poetry and wisdom. Odin values knowledge above all—he even sacrificed an eye to gain greater wisdom and insight into the future. Odin sits on the High Seat in Asgard and watches all that happens in the Nine Worlds. His two ravens, Hugin and Munin, help keep him informed. They fly throughout the worlds and report back with what they have seen and heard. Two wolves, Geri and Freki, also keep him company. Odin rides a swift eight-legged horse named Sleipnir, and he wields Gungnir, a magical spear that never misses its mark. Husband to the goddess Frigg, Odin is the father of many gods and goddesses, including Baldur, Thor, Hodur, Hermod, and Vali.

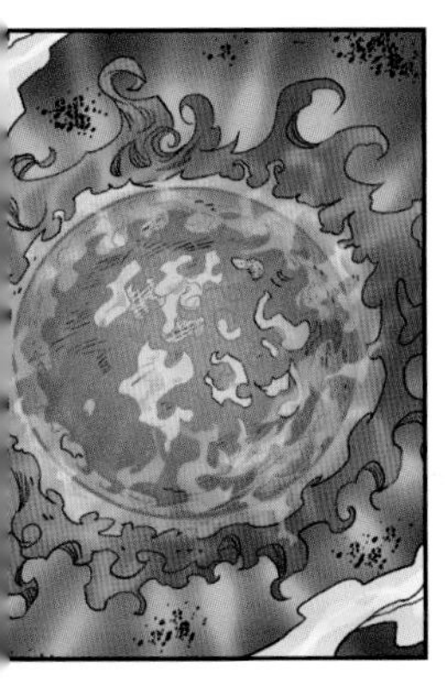

RAGNARÖK (RAHG-nuh-rok)—The great, final battle that brings the world to an end. Also known as the Twilight of the Gods and the Doom of the Gods. The death of the god Baldur is the first sign that Ragnarök is beginning. A series of cataclysmic events follow—families fight families, winter lasts for three years, the wolves Sköll and Hati devour the sun and moon, and the great wolf Fenrir and his father, the trickster Loki, are set free. At the sound of Heimdall's horn, the chief god Odin leads the Aesir and the forces of good to Vigrid, a wide field. There, they face Loki, an army of giants, and monsters of the underworld. Surt, a ferocious fire giant, sets the Nine Worlds aflame with his fiery blade. Almost all perish. But a human couple and a small number of gods survive Ragnarök, and a new, better, world will arise.

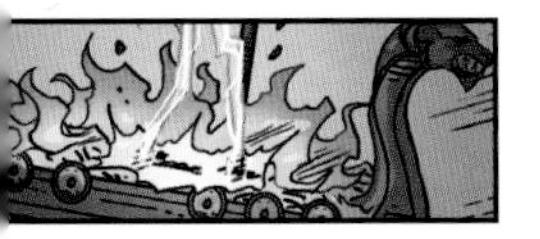

RINGHORN (RING-hawrn)—The ship that belongs to the god Baldur and is the largest of all the gods' vessels. However, the mighty ship does not sail the seas for long—it becomes a funeral pyre for the beloved god and his wife.

SESSRUMNIR (SESS-room-neer)—The hall of the goddess Freya, located in Asgard. Sessrumnir is not just the home of the love goddess. Freya also welcomes the souls of fallen warriors into her hall. Other warriors go to Valhalla, the hall of the chief god, Odin.

SIF (SIF)—The golden-haired goddess and wife of Thor. The trickster Loki once cut off all of Sif's hair. When Thor found out, he forced Loki to replace it. So Loki gave Sif a wig of gold strands that were crafted by dwarves and could grow like real hair.

SIGYN (SEE-gin)—A goddess and one of the wives of the trickster Loki. Even after the gods capture and chain Loki for his treachery, Sigyn remains by his side. She sits by Loki and uses a bowl to catch the venom that drips on him, giving Loki temporary relief from the searing pain of the poison.

SKADI (SKAH-dee)—A frost giantess known for her cold heart. She helps the Aesir punish Loki by placing a poisonous snake above the trickster's head so its venom will drip onto his eyes and cause him great pain.

SKÖLL (SKOHL)—A giant wolf that devours the sun at Ragnarök, the final battle. A second wolf, Hati, eats the moon.

SKRYMIR (SKREE-meer)—The truly massive giant that Thor, Loki, and Thialfi meet on the road to Jötunheim. He is so large that the group mistake one of his gloves for a cave. But after the visit to Utgard, the trio discover that the enormous giant was actually an illusion created by the giant king Utgarda-Loki.

SLEIPNIR (SLAYP-neer)—The eight-legged horse that belongs to the chief god, Odin. Sleipnir was a gift from the trickster Loki to Odin. The horse can travel over water and through the air. On land, he is faster than any other steed.

SURT (SURT)—The savage fire giant who leads a legion of warriors from Muspelheim, the land of fire, against the gods at Ragnarök, the final battle. Wielding his fiery sword, Surt sets the Nine Worlds aflame and reduces all to cinders.

THIALFI (thee-YAHL-fee)—The young human servant to the god Thor. The mortal son of a simple farmer, Thialfi is tricked into disobeying Thor's orders. To make amends he accompanies and helps the god during his adventures.

THOKK (THOK)—The giantess who refuses to weep for the dead god Baldur. In doing so, she prevents Baldur's release from the underworld. But what the Aesir do not realize, however, is that Thokk is actually the trickster Loki, using his shape-shifting skills to deceive them.

THOR (THOR)—The quick-tempered god of thunder and lightning. He is the son of the chief god, Odin, and husband of the goddess Sif. Thor is the mightiest of all the Aesir. With his magical war hammer, Mjölnir, Thor can call lightning from the sky to defend Asgard from its enemies. He wears unbreakable iron gloves and a legendary belt that doubles his godly might. When he travels throughout the Nine Worlds, Thor rides a chariot pulled by two goats, Toothgnasher and Toothgrinder. He is also frequently accompanied by his young human servant, Thialfi. Not always the wisest or cleverest of the gods, Thor loves grand feasts and slaying giants. He is well liked by the gods and worshipped by humans for the protection he provides against wicked giants and evil monsters.

THRYM (THRIM)—The king of the frost giants. His mind is set on getting the most precious treasure he can imagine—the heart of Freya, goddess of love and beauty. Thrym steals Thor's war hammer, Mjölnir, in hopes of forcing Freya to be his bride.

TYR (TAY-uhr)—A god of war who is known for being the bravest and most fair-minded of all the Aesir.

UTGARD (OOT-gahrd)—A stronghold in Jötunheim, the land of the giants. Utgard is ruled by the clever giant king Utgarda-Loki.

UTGARDA-LOKI (OOT-gahrd-ah-LOH-kee)—The clever giant king who rules over Utgard, a stronghold in Jötunheim, the land of giants. Utgarda-Loki uses cunning and magic to trick and humiliate the Aesir.

VALHALLA (val-HAL-uh)—A hall in Asgard built by the chief god, Odin, to house the souls of warriors and heroes who are killed in battle. There, the warriors spar and fight all day and feast all night. At Ragnarök, these honored dead join the Aesir in the fight against the giants and forces of evil.

VALI (VAHR-lee)—The youngest son of the chief god, Odin. Vali avenges the death of his half-brother Baldur by striking down the blind god, Hodur.

VIDAR (VEE-dahr)—The silent god and son of the chief god, Odin. At Ragnarök, when Odin falls in battle, Vidar viciously avenges his father. He then becomes the leader of the new gods when the world is restored.

VIGRID (VEE-grid)—The vast field on which the bloody battle of Ragnarök is fought.

VIKINGS—Norse warriors who raided and plundered the coasts of Europe and the British Isles from late 700's to about 1100. These fierce and skilled sailors came from Scandinavia, which includes modern day Denmark, Norway, and Sweden.

YGGDRASIL (IG-druh-sil)—The enormous ash tree in Norse mythology that spreads across the universe. Also called the World Tree, it binds together all of the Nine Worlds—holding up the worlds of gods, giants, dwarves, elves, and humans within its mighty branches and roots.

ABOUT THE RETELLING AUTHORS

CARL BOWEN is a father, husband, and writer living in Lawrenceville, Georgia, by way of Alexandria, Louisiana, and RAF Alconbury in Cambridgeshire, England. His works include graphic novel retellings of classic sci-fi tales, original comics set in the world of freestyle BMX riding and high school football, and a far-out twist on the classic "Jack and the Beanstalk" story. He's also the author of the Firestormers series and the *Kirkus* star-reviewed Shadow Squadron series. As of this writing, Carl has yet to try fighting giants with a magical war hammer.

LOUISE SIMONSON enjoys writing about monsters, science fiction, fantasy characters,and superheroes. She has authored the award-winning Power Pack series, several best-selling X-Men titles, the Web of Spider-Man series for Marvel Comics, and the Superman: Man of Steel series for DC Comics. She has also written many books for kids. Louise is married to comic artist and writer Walter Simonson and lives in the suburbs of New York City.

MICHAEL DAHL is the prolific author of the critically acclaimed Troll Hunters adventure series and more than 200 other books for children and young adults. He has won the AEP Distinguished Achievement Award three times for his nonfiction and has been short-listed twice by the Agatha Awards for his mysteries for young readers. Dahl currently lives in Minneapolis, Minnesota, a northern realm favorable to both trolls and Norse gods.

ABOUT THE ILLUSTRATORS

EDUARDO GARCIA is a passionate comic book fan and artist who works out of his studio (Red Wolf Studio) in Mexico City with the help of his talented son Sebastian Iñaki. He has brought his talent, pencils, and colors to varied projects for many titles and publishers such as Scooby-Doo (DC Comics), Spiderman Family (Marvel Comics), Flash Gordon (Aberdeen), and Speed Racer (IDW).

TOD SMITH is a self-employed illustrator and a graduate of the Joe Kubert School of Cartooning and Graphic Art. He has illustrated a wide variety of books, including work for Marvel Comics. He currently lives in Hartford, Connecticut.

REX LOKUS has been working in the comics industry for more than ten years and has been hired by companies such as Marvel Comics, DC Comics, Capstone, Wizuale (Poland), and FuryLion Studios (Russia). He has also worked on various independent projects.